VULGAR THE VIKING AND A MIDSUMMER NIGHT'S SCREAM

LOOK OUT FOR MORE
STORIES OF MAYHEM
AND CHAOS IN

VULGAR THE VIKING
AND THE ROCK CAKE RAIDERS

VULGAR THE VIKING
AND THE GREAT GULP GAMES

VULGAR THE VIKING
AND THE SPOOKY SCHOOL TRIP

VULGAR THE VIKING
AND THE TERRIBLE TALENT SHOW

VULGAR THE VIKING AND A MIDSUMMER NIGHT'S SCREAM

ODIN REDBEARD

ILLUSTRATED BY
SARAH HORNE

nosy
crow

With special thanks to
Barry Hutchison

First published in the UK in 2013 by Nosy Crow Ltd
The Crow's Nest, 10a Lant St
London, SE1 1QR, UK

Nosy Crow and associated logos are trademarks and/or
registered trademarks of Nosy Crow Ltd

Text copyright © Hothouse Fiction, 2013
Illustrations © Sarah Horne, 2013

The right of Hothouse Fiction and Sarah Horne to be identified as the author
and illustrator respectively of this work has been asserted by them in accordance
with the Copyright, Designs and Patents Act 1988.

A CIP catalogue record for this book will be available from the British Library

Printed and bound in the UK by Clays Ltd, St Ives Plc

Papers used by Nosy Crow are made from wood grown in sustainable forests.

ISBN: 978 0 85763 203 6

www.nosycrow.com

CHAPTER ONE

GUESSING GAME

The morning sun danced into Vulgar's bedroom and tickled his eyes open. A chorus of tweeting birds welcomed a brand-new day, as the smell of the hayfields wafted in through his window.

After weeks of rain, summer had finally arrived in the Viking village of Blubber, and Vulgar wasn't about to waste a minute of it!

1

He jumped out of bed, tripped over a bundle of fur and fell face-first on to the floor. The bundle of fur raised its head and gave a grumpy *woof*.

"Sorry, Grunt," said Vulgar, hopping back to his feet. "Didn't smell you there."

Vulgar went to the window and looked out. The sky was a brilliant blue with not a cloud in sight. The sun burned just above the horizon, turning the distant ocean into a lake of fire.

It was the perfect day for pillaging. Then again, it was *always* the perfect day for pillaging as far as Vulgar was concerned. He just wished the rest of the village felt the same way.

Many of the villagers were outside now, digging their gardens and watering their flowers. Some of them were tending to their vegetable patches. Vulgar shuddered. In his opinion, real Vikings didn't bother with *vegetables*.

Vulgar stretched and patted down his wild, greasy hair. He rubbed his chin and was disappointed to discover he still didn't have a beard. Proper Vikings needed beards, and he wished his would hurry up and arrive.

A deep, rumbling sound suddenly shook the room around him. He turned and looked at his dog. "Grunt, was that you?

What *have* you been eating?"

The sound came again, louder this time than before, and Vulgar realised it wasn't coming from the dog. It was a truly horrible noise, deep and booming, but with a nasty high-pitched whine at the edges. He imagined it was what an angry whale with indigestion would sound like.

He hoped it might be an invading army, or a crazed dragon, but nothing that exciting ever happened in Blubber.

The sound reached an ear-splitting high note that made his whole skeleton tremble, and Vulgar finally realised what it was.

His mum was singing.

"Morning, my little turnip," said Helga, as Vulgar shuffled into the kitchen.

"Morning." He watched her twirl around the table. It was like watching an elk try to do ballet. "You look cheerful."

"Of course I am, my darling walrus whisker!" Helga cried. She wrapped her arms around Vulgar and gave him a hug.

6

He felt like a stick insect trying to wrestle a bear. "Tomorrow is Midsummer's Eve!"

Vulgar slipped back down on to the floor and took a seat at the table. He tore himself a chunk of bread and popped it in his mouth. "Oh, great. Already?" he asked, spraying crumbs everywhere.

"Try to sound a bit happier about it," said Helga. "It's the most exciting day of the Viking year!"

Vulgar's dad appeared in the doorway. Harald's thin, wispy beard was caked in mud. At least, Vulgar hoped it was mud.

His dad cleaned toilets for a living and you never knew what might end up stuck in his beard.

"Midsummer's Eve!" Harald cheered.

"Midsummer's Eve!" Helga replied. They hugged, and for a moment Harald was lost somewhere in his wife's powerful arms.

"Ooh, careful dear," Harald groaned. "My back's not what it used to be."

Helga released her grip and Harald took a seat beside his son.

"Why are you so excited?" Vulgar asked. "Midsummer's Eve is rubbish. It's all dancing around the maypole and stuff."

"And the choosing of the Midsummer's King and Queen," Helga reminded him.

"Oh well, that makes it better," said Vulgar, even though he didn't really think so. Queens and dancing were his second and third least favourite things in the world. Maypoles were his first.

"Here, remember when I was picked as the Midsummer Queen?" said Helga. "All those years ago. Dancing round the maypole…"

Harald smiled fondly at the memory. "All those potholes you left in the village green. The screams of panic when we all thought the ground was going to crack open…"

Vulgar cackled at the thought of his mum thudding around the maypole. Helga shot him a dirty look.

"I don't know what you're laughing at," she said. "It's time you went to school!"

"Right, you lot, quit yakkin' an' listen up."

Vulgar glanced across at his best friend, Knut. Knut was much taller than Vulgar, and as skinny as a rake. He looked as if someone had taken a normal-sized boy and stretched him. He sat slumped in his seat, his messy hair poking out from beneath his lopsided helmet, staring at the man at the front of the class.

Vulgar followed his gaze. The bony figure with the long grey beard wasn't their teacher, it was Harrumf, steward of the Great Hall and personal assistant to…

11

"The high-uppiest of highnesses," announced Harrumf, waggling his walking stick at the class. "The kingliest of kings. The right regal royal, Kiiiiiing Olaf!"

A muted applause rippled around the class, then faded quickly. Only Princess Freya, King Olaf's daughter, continued to clap.

Princess Freya was the closest thing Vulgar had to an enemy. She looked sweet enough, with her long blonde plaits and delicate features, but she fought dirty when no one was looking, and the person she liked to fight most was Vulgar.

King Olaf's beard appeared in the doorway, followed by his stomach. The rest of him came strutting through the door a little while later, doing his best royal wave.

"Thank you, thank you," he said. "Too kind. Too kind."

Freya stopped clapping and silence fell over the classroom. "I expect you're wondering why you're all here," King Olaf boomed.

"To learn stuff," Vulgar said.

King Olaf nodded. "Right, yes. It's school. I forgot about that. Then I suspect you're wondering why *I'm* here."

Knut raised a hand.

"Yes?"

"Are you lost?"

The king frowned. "What? No, I…"

"I get lost sometimes," said Knut.

"He does," agreed Vulgar. "He got lost in his own house once."

"Well, I'm not lost," said King Olaf.

"Took a whole day to find him," Vulgar added. "My dog had to sniff him out in the end. Tell him where you were, Knut."

14

"I was under my blankets."

"Can anyone tell me why we celebrate Midsummer's Eve?" said King Olaf, cutting Vulgar off.

"Is it a kind of punishment?" Vulgar guessed.

"No! It's because when the days are at their longest, the trolls and elves and other spirits come out to cause mischief."

Vulgar thought about this. "What sort of mischief?"

"Oh, you know," said King Olaf. "Just… general mischief."

"Like putting itching berries down people's backs?" Vulgar asked.

"Yes. Just like that!"

"And filling their pockets with elk manure?" asked Knut.

King Olaf puffed out his cheeks. "Yes. Well. I suppose they might…"

"Oh! Oh!" yelped Vulgar, bouncing in his seat. "And tying girls' pig tails to trees then filling their shoes with frogspawn?"

16

Princess Freya gave Vulgar a nasty glare and stuck her tongue out. Vulgar grinned at her.

"Possibly, possibly," said King Olaf, nodding. "So that's why we have the Midsummer's Eve celebrations – with a big bonfire in the square to scare off the wicked spirits."

Vulgar's eyes lit up. How could he have forgotten about the bonfire? Bonfires were *brilliant*! Maybe Midsummer's Eve wasn't going to be so bad after all!

17

"Also, we hold the traditional maypole dance to ensure that Blubber has a good harvest. This year, one very lucky boy will be named Midsummer King and will dance with my darling daughter!"

Or maybe it was.

Vulgar leaned over to Knut. "I'd rather dance with one of the trolls," he whispered.

"I imagine you're all desperate to dance with Freya." King Olaf beamed.

"Wow," Knut whispered. "He's

certainly got a good imagination."

"And so, to make it fair, every boy will guess how many dragons I have slain in my life so far. The boy who guesses the closest will be crowned the Midsummer King."

Vulgar's mind raced. He *really* didn't want to dance with Freya. He came up with a plan. He'd guess a really high number and make sure he was nowhere near the real figure.

"Six," said one boy.

King Olaf shook his head. "No."

"Fourteen," guessed another.

"Wrong."

"None?" offered Knut.

King Olaf shuffled uneasily and gave a little laugh. "Haha. Don't be silly."

"Eight hundred and forty-seven!" cried Vulgar.

King Olaf pointed at him. "Yes!" he

said. "Bang on. I've killed *exactly* eight hundred and forty-seven dragons!"

"Ooooh," said the class, who were obviously impressed.

Vulgar's eyes went wide with horror. "What? But… I mean…?"

"Congratulations, my boy," boomed King Olaf.

Vulgar looked round and met Freya's gaze. The princess smirked at him. "Well done… *Your Highness.*"

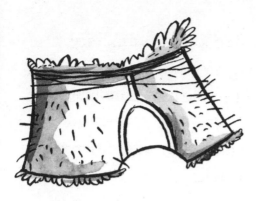

CHAPTER TWO

PRACTICE MAKES TERRIBLE

That afternoon, when school was over, Vulgar crawled beneath the tables. He was heading for the door, ready to make a run for it as soon as he was outside. He crept on. Almost there...

A pair of shoes stepped up to the end of the table and blocked his way. "Don't think you can escape that easily," Freya said. She ducked her head under the table. "Come out. Stop hiding."

Vulgar plodded forward on his hands and knees. "I wasn't hiding," he said, standing up. "I... dropped a bogey."

Freya's fine features wrinkled in disgust. "I beg your pardon?"

"It's my favourite one. I've been keeping it for weeks." He waved to Knut, who was lurking just outside the door.

"Anyway, can't stop, I have to catch up with Knut."

"Oh no you don't," said Freya, catching him by the back of his tunic. "We have to rehearse our maypole dance."

"Hooray!" cheered Vulgar, then he slapped his forehead. "Oh, wait a minute, I forgot. I can't. I've got homework to do."

"No, you don't," Freya snapped.

"How do you know?"

"Because I'm in your class, Vulgar. Remember?"

Vulgar's shoulders sagged. "Oh yeah, so you are. Well then, I have to… have to…"

"Walk your dog," whispered Knut. The whisper was so loud Freya heard every word.

"Yes!" said Vulgar. "I need to walk my

dog. Such a shame. I was really looking forward to dancing with you, Freya."

"Were you?" said Knut. "Oh, right. Well, I'll take Grunt for a walk, then."

Vulgar went pale. "No, Knut, wait!"

But Knut had already left. Vulgar turned to find Freya grinning at him. Vulgar thought fast. "I just remembered, I have to—"

"Nice try, Vulgar," the princess said. She grabbed him by the arm and hauled him out of the school. "But I'm not falling for it. You're dancing with me, and that's final!"

They made their way towards the Great Hall. Freya skipped and hopped with excitement. Vulgar dragged out every last step, trailing his feet along the ground.

"Just wait until you see me dance. I move like a swan," Freya boasted.

24

Vulgar frowned. "What, waddling around on your stumpy little legs?"

Freya punched him on the arm. "That's not what I meant and you know it."

They turned a corner that led on to the square. Vulgar groaned when he saw the Great Hall. It had been covered in colourful ribbons and bunches of flowers. It wasn't likely to scare off an enemy army, unless they had hayfever.

"Come on," Freya urged. "My dad and your mum are waiting for us inside."

Vulgar shuffled on for a few more steps, then came to a halt. "Wait… did you say my mum? What's she doing here?"

"Didn't you know?" asked Freya. She smiled sweetly. "Your mum is going to help my dad demonstrate the maypole dance."

Vulgar shuddered at the thought of his mum thudding around the hall with King Olaf. "*Oh no!*" he said, but Freya caught his arm and pulled him up the steps that led into the hall.

"Ah, here come our king and queen to rehearse their dance," boomed King Olaf, as Vulgar and Freya entered. He winked. "Ready to see how the experts do it?"

"Yes, please!" cheered Freya.

"Do we have to?" groaned Vulgar, but his mum and King Olaf ignored him. They stood at opposite sides of a wooden pole that was positioned in the centre of the hall. Long pink and white ribbons hung down from the pole which was topped with flowers.

The maypole was shorter than Vulgar had imagined it would be. And thinner, too.

"Your silly maypole is more like a may*twig*," he whispered to Freya scornfully, who stuck her tongue out at him.

Harrumf gave him a dirty look. "None of your nonsense, boy. It's plenty big enough!" And the elderly viking shuffled crossly to the back of the hall.

Helga and the king took hold of a ribbon each, then bowed to one another.

Harrumf set down his walking stick and picked up a large net with a long wooden handle.

"Ready, my queen?" asked King Olaf. Helga smiled and fluttered her eyelashes.

"Oh yes, my king, your queen is ready," she said, and she gave a little giggle. Vulgar felt himself blush with embarassment.

And then the dancing started. Vulgar only knew it was dancing because they'd said so in advance. It was like no dancing he'd ever seen before.

They both thundered around the maypole like warring walruses, their bodies wobbling as they twirled and spun clumsily around and around. *BOOM-BOOM-BOOM* went their feet until the very hall began to shake.

From the corner of his eye, Vulgar saw Harrumf move. The old man shot forward with the net, catching a metal plate just as it shuddered off a shelf. He lay it on the floor, then lunged again as a set of antlers came toppling down off the wall.

"You are as fleet-footed as a reindeer, my queen!" cried Olaf, as he and Helga

31

stomped faster
and faster around the pole.

"And you are as graceful as a mighty
elk, my king," laughed Helga.

Vulgar went from red to green. "I think
I'm going to be sick," he mumbled. Helga
did a little skip and Harrumf had to dive
to catch an ornamental shield before it

could smash against the floor.

After a few more steps, a final twirl, and one or two broken floorboards, Helga and King Olaf stopped dancing. They bowed to one another again, puffing and panting heavily, then turned to the children and grinned.

"There," said Helga. "That's how it's done!"

At the back of the hall, Harrumf swapped the net for his walking stick and hobbled away, muttering under his breath.

"Shall we leave the youngsters to it?" suggested Olaf. He gallantly held out an arm and Helga linked her own arm through it. "Practise well. Remember – the whole village will be watching you tomorrow night."

"Don't remind me," Vulgar sighed. He watched his mum and King Olaf skip out of the hall, then turned to Freya. "OK, they're gone. Let's make a run for it."

"Ha!" Freya snapped, "I don't think so. Grab a ribbon."

Vulgar thought about arguing, but Freya was making a face that said arguing would be a silly idea. He took hold of a white ribbon and held it between one finger and thumb. "There. Happy?"

"Very. Now I hope you were paying attention to their dancing."

Vulgar shook his head. "I had my eyes closed for most of it."

Freya tutted. "Well, it's lucky for you that I know what I'm doing. Now copy me and try not to fall over."

The princess bowed. Vulgar hesitated, then he rolled his eyes and bowed in return. His helmet hit the maypole with a *clonk*. "Ow!"

Freya sighed. "This could be a long afternoon," she said, then she started to dance. Her movements were smooth and graceful, her arms looping out, the ribbon fluttering in her hand.

Vulgar wasn't quite so graceful. He hopped and clattered around the pole, the horns of his helmet tangling in the dangling ribbons.

"Be careful, or you're going to pull the whole thing down," Freya warned.

"Oh, wouldn't that be a shame?" said Vulgar. He gave the maypole a nudge with his shoulder, but it didn't budge. So he thudded into Freya, knocking them both to the ground.

"Do you work hard to be this useless, or does it just come naturally?" she said, pushing him away with a scowl. They got back up and she made him try again.

"Lift your leg," Freya barked. "No, the other leg. Now spin around. Not that way! You're like a three-legged moose with its head in a bucket. This is hopeless. Can't you move any faster?"

Faster? thought Vulgar. *I'll show you faster!*

He grabbed hold of another few ribbons and began to run around the maypole at top speed. He scrambled past Freya and the ribbons looped around her.

"Careful," she warned. "You're getting me tangled up!"

"That's the idea," Vulgar said, laughing. He ran faster still, grabbing another ribbon and wrapping it around Freya and the maypole.

He was dizzy by the time he stopped, but he didn't mind. Freya was now tied tightly to the maypole by a dozen or more lengths of ribbon. Vulgar grinned from ear to ear.

"There," he said. "Was *that* fast enough for you?"

"Untie me, Vulgar," Freya hissed. "Right now!"

"Good luck finding a new king, *Your Highness*," Vulgar said. Smirking, he gave her one final bow, then with a whoop of delight, he turned and ran through the door and out of the Great Hall.

CHAPTER THREE

KEPT IN THE CASTLE

Vulgar ran from the Great Hall and
dashed across the village green. He had
done it. He was free! Now to find some
proper Viking stuff to do.

It didn't take him long to find Knut.
His friend was at the edge of the village
trying to carry a bundle of sticks. He was
dropping most of them, and every time
he bent to pick one up more would fall to

the ground.

"Hello!" cried Vulgar.

Knut gave a yelp and dropped the rest of his sticks. He stared at Vulgar in surprise. "I thought you were supposed to be dancing?"

Vulgar shrugged. "I told Freya that real Vikings don't dance around maypoles. She said I could go."

Knut looked puzzled and scratched one of the horns on his helmet. "Really?"

"Nah," Vulgar said with a grin. "I tied her up and ran away. What are you doing?"

"Collecting sticks for the bonfire."

Vulgar's eyes lit up. "*Thor's teeth!* I'd

forgotten about the bonfire." He leapt into action and began pushing the fallen wood into a pile. "We're going to need a lot more than that," he said.

"I don't think they want too much," Knut said. "It isn't going to be a very big bonfire."

"*What?*" spluttered Vulgar. "Says who?"

Knut shrugged. "The grown-ups. They're worried a big bonfire might be dangerous."

"Of course it will be dangerous!" Vulgar cried. "That's the whole point! Vikings eat danger for breakfast!"

"Really?" said Knut, frowning. "My mum gives me oatmeal."

"I've tasted your mum's cooking," said Vulgar. "Trust me – it's dangerous." He pushed sticks into the pile. "Let's get some more wood. We're going to make this the biggest bonfire Blubber has ever seen. It'll be so big it'll melt the snow on the mountains! They'll be able to see it at the North Pole!"

The boys spent the next hour gathering sticks and branches from the woods outside the village. Some of the branches were too big for them to carry, but they heaved and dragged them over to their ever-growing pile.

As Knut dropped a large branch on to the stack, Vulgar leapt out from the woods, a long spiky stick held in one hand. He waggled it around like a sword.

"Halt, lowly dog! It is I, Thrunt Mangleson, leader of the Viking

horde. Face me in combat
or… or…"

"Or what?" asked Knut.

"Or I'll have your arms
off," growled Vulgar. He
swished his play sword
around to prove his point.

Thrunt Mangleson was one
of Vulgar's all-time Viking
heroes. He had led an army
of Vikings in an attack on the
town of Lumpp, far across the sea
in Angle Land. The Vikings came
with swords, shields, axes and a
great big hammer with spikes
on the end. The Lumppian
townsfolk had spades and
frying pans, and wore
wooden buckets as helmets.
It went down in history as
"The Seven-Minute War".

"Very well, Mangleson," said Knut, grabbing a stick from the pile. "Challenge accepted!"

The boys laughed as they began *clacking* their sticks together in battle. The pretend swords swished and sliced through the air as they thrust and parried around the woodpile.

Suddenly Vulgar heard a war cry from behind him. He turned sharply, his sword raised, ready to face whatever horrible creature had crept up on him. A huge dark shadow passed across him, and Vulgar's face went pale.

"Mum?"

Helga reached down and lifted Vulgar up by the tunic.

Vulgar
heard a giggle
coming from
behind his mum. Freya
stepped out from behind
Helga's back, stuck her
tongue out at Vulgar,
then smiled sweetly.

"Did you tie the
princess up?" Helga demanded.

"No!" said Vulgar. His mum
growled at him. "Well…
maybe a bit."

"Apologise,"
said Helga.

"But…"

"Say. Sorry.
Now!"

Vulgar wanted to argue, but his mum could be scary when she wanted to, and now she *really* wanted to. "Sorry," he mumbled, then he gave an *oof* as Helga let him drop to the ground. "Since you've missed out on so much rehearsal time, you're going to stay at the castle until the festivities tomorrow so you can practise," Helga said. Vulgar opened his mouth to complain, but his mum shot him that look again.

"All right," he grumbled. He dropped his stick, waved a sad goodbye to Knut, then trudged after his mum and Freya all the way to King Olaf's castle.

Vulgar didn't mind the castle. It had suits of armour and swords and tapestries about battles. He just didn't like the fact that Freya lived there.

"Midsummer Kings need to have perfect manners," the princess said. "It's dinner soon, so I want you to use your napkin properly."

Vulgar blinked. "What's a napkin?"

"It stops your food landing in your lap," Freya explained.

47

"Oh. My dog usually does that."

Freya sighed. "You tuck it into your tunic or lay it across your lap. As you eat, you can also use it to dab the corners of your mouth. But dab. Don't wipe. Kings never wipe."

Vulgar thought about this. "What, even after they've been to the—?"

"*Vulgar!*" Freya yelped. "Don't be so... so... *vulgar*. Go and wash your hands."

"They're not dirty," said Vulgar. He looked at the black dirt beneath his fingernails. "No more than usual, anyway."

"Go," said Freya, pointing to the bathroom. "And use soap!"

"*Soap?* But..."

"Do you want me to call your mum back here?"

Vulgar bit his lip before he could say anything else. With a sigh he turned and trudged into the bathroom.

"And scrub properly," ordered Freya.
"I'll be checking them carefully."

After three attempts, Vulgar's hands
were clean enough for Freya's liking.
She led him through to the dining room,
where a huge table was laid out with
more food than he had ever seen in his
life.

King Olaf was sitting at the head of the
table, already munching his way through
a whole chicken. Vulgar raced to the
table and grabbed for some pickled whale
meat, but Freya slapped his hand.

"Manners," she said. "A king doesn't eat with his hands."

Vulgar pointed to Freya's father. "*He* does!"

"Yes, well, you don't!" She passed him a fork and tossed him a napkin. "Your mum said you had to do what I told you, remember?"

"No, she didn't!"

"Yes, she did," sniffed Freya. "You obviously weren't listening."

Reluctantly, Vulgar tucked in his napkin and speared some food with the fork. King Olaf was now tearing into a

whole leg of roast elk, using his fingers to get at the juicy bits.

"Tell me about the evil spirits that come on Midsummer's night," Vulgar said.

Olaf wiped – not dabbed – his mouth on the back of his sleeve. "Oh, they're nasty things," he said. "Trolls... um... other things."

"Ogres?" asked Vulgar.

"Hmm? Oh yes. Yes. Definitely ogres. Nothing worse than ogres."

"Have you ever met an ogre?" Vulgar asked.

Olaf snorted. "One? I've met two hundred of them! An entire ogre army once attacked me in the woods. It's lucky I had my sword, otherwise I could've been in real trouble."

"Did you defeat them all?" gasped Vulgar.

King Olaf smoothed down his beard.

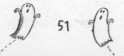

"Put it this way – they don't call it 'Dead Ogre Wood' for nothing."

Vulgar frowned. "But nobody does call it that."

The king frowned. "Yes. Well. Maybe they should start."

"What other evil spirits come out? Sprites?"

"Of course."

"Elves?"

"Almost certainly." King Olaf nodded. "Mischievous beggars, elves."

Vulgar looked sideways at Freya. She had eaten her main course and was about to start on dessert. Vulgar wasn't sure what it was, but it had strawberries and blueberries and thick dollops of cream. It looked delicious.

"Look – an elf!" he cried and he pointed into the corner of the dining room. Freya and Olaf looked in the direction he had pointed, giving him just enough time to scoop a handful of Freya's pudding and cram it in his mouth.

He swallowed just as Freya turned back. "Hey, what happened to my pudding?" she squealed.

Vulgar grinned. There were little bits of strawberry between his teeth. "Must have been the elf," he said.

Freya's eyes narrowed. "It's not elves you need to be afraid of," she said.

"I'm not afraid of anything," Vulgar replied.

"Good. Then you won't be scared of the castle ghosts."

"Ghosts?"

"Oh yes!" boomed King Olaf. "The place is full of them. Old King Godfred the Ghastly is the worst. Legend says he used to chop people up and have them for dinner. Sometimes when the castle is quiet you can hear him pacing the corridors, sharpening his axe and growling like a wild animal."

"Growling?" whispered Vulgar.

"Yes," said Freya. "But that won't bother you. *You're* not afraid of anything."

That night, Vulgar lay wide awake in bed. The guest bedroom he'd been put in was nice. That was the problem. It was *too* nice. It didn't shake with his mum's snoring. It didn't smell of stinky dog. When he couldn't sleep at home he'd count the fleas on his covers, but there were no fleas anywhere to be found.

And he was also worried about Godfred the Ghastly. Was he out there somewhere, pacing the corridors and sharpening his axe?

Vulgar gulped. That did it. He'd never get to sleep now. There was only one thing for it – he had to sneak home to his own bed.

He tiptoed to the bedroom door. It gave a *creak* as he eased it open. He held his breath and peeped out into the corridor. A single torch was burning in a holder on the wall.

It cast spooky shadows across the stone.
Being careful not to make a sound,
Vulgar crept out into the corridor. The
flickering flame of the torch made the
shadows move and for a moment
he thought he saw a little elf
darting through the
darkness.

He froze, then
almost laughed when the
shape gave a soft *squeak*.
"Just a mouse," he whispered,
tiptoeing on.
The safest way out of the castle would

probably be through the kitchen door at the back. Vulgar made his way in that direction, sneaking along the corridor and creeping down the stone steps.

The corridor leading to the kitchen was almost completely dark. There was no torch burning here, and the moonlight coming in through the narrow windows did little to lift the gloom.

Vulgar was halfway along the passageway before he saw it – the shadow of a figure with a horned helmet blocking the back door. The figure let out a snorting grunt that made Vulgar's heart pound faster. It sounded like the growling of a wild animal.

King Godfred the Ghastly had found him!

CHAPTER FOUR

GHOST BUSTER

Vulgar held his breath and slowly backed away from the ghostly figure, looking for something to defend himself with. He thought about running away, but proper Vikings never ran away. They faced danger head on.

He gave a soft whimper. For the first time ever he *really* wished he didn't want to be a proper Viking.

The door to the kitchen was on his right. He ducked in there and searched for a weapon, but all the sharp things had been safely locked out of reach.

There was a large iron cooking pot sitting on one of the worktops. Vulgar tried lifting it, but it was too heavy to budge. He decided just to take the lid instead and use it as a shield.

Over in the corner, a broom was propped against the wall. Its handle was longer and heavier than the stick he'd fought Knut with, and he reckoned even a ghost wouldn't want to be thumped on the head with it.

He poked his head back out into the corridor, hoping the ghost would be gone. No such luck. The shadow was still there, growling and grunting away. Vulgar crept out of the kitchen. Maybe if he took the ghost by surprise he would have a better chance of defeating it. Carefully – ever so carefully – he crept along the corridor.

"I'm going to eat you up!" the ghost said, smacking its lips together.

That did it. Godfred the Ghastly's ghost had seen him. There was no way to surprise it now. There was only one thing left to do.

"CHAAAAAARGE!" yelled Vulgar, raising the broom handle above his head and running for the shadowy shape. He brought the stick down sharply. It hit with a *whang* on the top of a horned helmet.

The ghostly figure seemed to grow to twice its size. "Ooyah," it grunted. "Me bleedin' 'ead."

Vulgar swung again, this time cracking the ghost across one leg. It gave another yelp and began to hop. "*Ow!*" cried the figure. "'Ere, cut that out!"

Something moved behind Vulgar. An even larger shape lunged at him from out of the darkness. Freya had been right. This place was crawling with ghosts! He would have to fight his way out! Vulgar swung with his broom handle and the shadow gave a loud "Ouch!"

With a Viking roar, Vulgar swung again in a big half-circle. He managed to hit both ghosts this time.

"Oof! Me back!"

"Argh! My knee! Stop that right now!"

Vulgar was about to swing again when he realised that both voices sounded familiar. *Very* familiar. A horrible sinking feeling began to swoosh around in his stomach.

A torch came round the corner, carried by a sleepy-looking Freya. The torch's flame pushed the darkness away, revealing Harrumf. He was rubbing his back and glaring angrily down at Vulgar.

"You!" he spat. "I might 'ave bleedin' known."

Vulgar smiled nervously, then turned to see King Olaf hopping up and down behind him. The king was wearing nothing but a long white nightdress and an angry expression.

"What *is* the meaning of this?" he demanded. "I come out to see what all the noise is and you start attacking me!"

"He attacked me an' all," Harrumf said. The old man's beard was full of crumbs, and he had half a meat pie in his hand.

"I thought you were a ghost," Vulgar explained. "I thought you were Godfred the Ghastly and you were going to eat me."

Freya giggled and Vulgar felt his cheeks blush red. "He said he was going to eat me up!"

Harrumf frowned. "No, I didn't."

"Yes, you did! You were grunting and growling and—"

"Snoring?" said King Olaf.

Harrumf shook his head. "What? Not me, Yer Majesty. Wide awake and on patrol, I was."

64

"So not asleep in that chair, then?" said King Olaf. He pointed to a chair propped against the wall, just where Vulgar had first seen the shadowy figure. "Halfway through eating that pie. Dreaming about… oh, I don't know… the Midsummer's Eve feast, perhaps?"

Harrumf fiddled nervously with the hem of his tunic. "Perish the thought, Yer High Royalness. Wouldn't catch me sleepin' on duty."

"I would and I have many times," King Olaf said. He waved a hand. "Still, no harm done, I suppose."

65

"Eh? What about me back?"

Olaf ignored him. "Back to bed, you two. Freya, show Vulgar the way to his room, would you? And, Vulgar, I want you to stay there until morning."

Vulgar's shoulders sagged. "Oh, all right."

Freya led him from the kitchen along the corridor towards his room. In the torchlight, Vulgar could see that her broad smile stretched from ear to ear. "Now you'll definitely have to dance around the maypole with me," she said.

"Oh yeah? How do you work that out?" Vulgar asked.

"Because if you don't," the princess said, giggling, "I'll tell everyone how terrified you are of ghosts!"

"You wouldn't," said Vulgar.

"Oh, I so would," said Freya. They stopped outside Vulgar's bedroom door.

"Goodnight. Be sure to get plenty of sleep. I want you rested for our dancing tomorrow." She smirked. "The whole village will be watching us, after all."

"Don't remind me," Vulgar groaned, then he crawled into bed, pulled the covers over his head, and tossed and turned until morning.

CHAPTER FIVE

BATTLE FOR THE CROWN

Just before seven o'clock the castle was invaded by musicians, cleaners, decorators, waiters, waitresses and chefs. By then, Vulgar had already been practising his maypole dancing for over an hour. He'd had to beg Princess Freya to let him stop for breakfast.

As Vulgar trudged to the kitchen, people raced by him in both directions.

68

They carried armfuls of bunting and
stacks of plates and huge racks of meat.

The smell of cooking food wafted along
the passageway and he followed his nose
down the steps and into the castle kitchen.
It looked completely different in daylight.
Cooks bustled around, roasting every
kind of delicacy under the sun.

Vulgar's stomach rumbled loudly. In fact, he'd never heard it rumble so loudly before. Then he realised the rumbling was coming from behind him. He turned to see his mum rolling an enormous barrel of mead into the kitchen. Another barrel was slung over her shoulder. She patted him on the head with her free hand as she passed.

"Morning! Sleep well?"

Vulgar yawned. "Not really." He looked around the kitchen. "What's for breakfast?"

"Don't you dare," Helga warned. "This food is for the feast tonight. You're not to touch any of it. Understood?"

Vulgar nodded, but then he spotted a plate of rock cakes cooling over on the table. There was another rumbling sound, and this time it really was his stomach. He waved goodbye to his

mum and waited for her to turn away.
The moment she did,
he shot under the table
and crawled forward
until he was directly
beneath the plate
of rock cakes.

He glanced
left and right.
Everyone in
the kitchen was
too busy to notice
him. He would only take one cake. Just
a small one. There were dozens of them
on that plate. It wasn't like anyone would
miss one little cake.

His hand shot up like a striking snake
and snatched a rock cake from the plate.
He gobbled it hungrily, even though
it was still a little bit on the hot side.
Vulgar's stomach rumbled again.

Two cakes. He would only take two cakes. Three at the very most.

His hand reached up again, but this time someone caught it by the wrist. He yelped as he was pulled out from beneath the table. Princess Freya glared down at him, still holding his wrist.

"Break's over! I've been looking everywhere for you. Come with me," she said.

"Where to?" asked Vulgar. "And can I have another cake?"

"Outside. And no, you can't." Her grip tightened on Vulgar's wrist. "You're going to help me pick flowers."

Vulgar tried to yank his arm away, but Freya held it tightly. "Pick flowers?" he gasped. "Vikings would rather die than pick flowers."

"Let's hope they don't come back as

ghosts, then, or you'd run away crying," Freya said. She opened her eyes wide and made a spooky *wooooooh* sound.

Vulgar gritted his teeth. "Fine. I'll come with you."

Freya handed him a basket and together they headed out into the gardens at the back of the castle.

"Ugh," he grimaced, as they stepped into the early morning sunshine. "What's that stink?"

Freya breathed deeply. "It's the smell of flowers, silly. Isn't it beautiful?"

Vulgar pinched his nose and pretended to be sick on the grass. Freya tutted. "Stop messing around and help me pick some."

The princess skipped across the garden, picking one or two stems from each flower bed. Vulgar found a long, thin stick sticking out of the soil. There was a tall sunflower tied to it, but Vulgar thought it was probably big enough to stand on its own now.

He untied the twine holding the flower to the stick. The sunflower immediately fell over. Vulgar pulled the stick out of the soil with a soft *plop*.

It *whummed* loudly when he swung it about. *Brilliant*, he thought, and

74

he set off following Freya, *whumming* the sword as he went. He wondered how Knut was getting on. Wherever he was, it had to be more fun than this.

Vulgar stopped when he spotted a scarecrow. It leaned on a post near a vegetable patch, its arms held out at its sides. The scarecrow was bigger than he was. An angry face had been painted on to its sackcloth head. It would make a worthy opponent.

"Have some of this," Vulgar cried, and the stick *whummed* through the air. It made a loud

smack as it struck the scarecrow's arm.
Vulgar drew back his make-believe sword
and growled. "Still standing, I see? Well,
maybe you'd like some of this! And some
of this! Or even some of this!"

Vulgar thwacked the scarecrow again
and again, until lumps of stuffing and
straw were flying all over the garden.
Still the scarecrow refused to surrender.

"You're a brave one, I'll give you that,"
Vulgar said. He was breathing heavily,
tired from his attack. "But let's see how
you cope with this!"

He brought the stick down hard on
the scarecrow's legs. There was a *crack*
from the wooden pole and the scarecrow
began to topple forward.

"Back, foul ogre!" Vulgar cried, but
it was no use. He gave a squeal as the
scarecrow crashed down, pinning him
to the ground. "Help!" he yelped.

"I told you to pick flowers," Freya said, looming over him. She lifted the scarecrow away and Vulgar scrambled to his feet. "Anyway, it doesn't matter," Freya continued. "I picked enough for both of us."

"Enough for what?"

"For these," said Freya. She held out a crown she'd made by weaving flower stems together.

Vulgar snorted. "Ha! What poor sap is going to wear that?"

Freya started at him. Vulgar's jaw dropped open.

"No. No way! I'm not wearing a crown made of flowers!" he gasped. "Dancing is bad enough."

"It's tradition," Freya said. "The Midsummer King and Queen always wear flower crowns."

"Not this year they don't," Vulgar insisted. "Anyway, I can't. I'm allergic to flowers." He faked a loud sneeze then jammed a finger up his nose and fished out a large green bogey. "See?"

"You're disgusting," Freya said, "but I don't believe you." She plonked the flowery crown on his head.

Vulgar ripped it off and threw it back at her. "I'm not wearing it."

Freya put the crown back on his head. "Yes, you are."

Vulgar tore it off again. "No, I'm not."

Freya threw herself forward and slammed her shoulder into Vulgar's stomach. They crashed down on to a bed of red flowers, flattening them all.

"You're wearing the crown!" Freya cried. She grabbed for it, but Vulgar twisted away and rolled across the soil.

"Not! Not! Not!" Vulgar shouted, then he spluttered when Freya rammed a handful of leaves into his mouth.

Freya raised her legs and Vulgar was sent flying over her head. He landed with a *splat*, face down in the flower bed. The princess caught hold of his foot and bent it so his heel was touching his bum.

Vulgar gave a yelp. "OK, fine, fine!" he cried. "I'll wear the stupid flower hat."

"Promise," said Freya.

"Promise!"

Freya hopped up, put the crowns back in her basket, then skipped back towards the castle. Vulgar trudged after her, limping slightly. He sighed. At least there was no way today could get any worse.

"You. Bath. Now," said Vulgar's mum when he hobbled into the kitchen.

Vulgar froze. He thought about turning and running, but he knew he couldn't outrun Helga. He'd once seen her chase down an elk after it had chewed through the washing line and run away with her massive pants hooked over its antlers.

"But I had a bath," Vulgar argued. "Last month. Remember? It had water in it and everything."

"And now you need another one," Helga said. "You're filthy."

Vulgar looked down at himself. His fight with Freya had left him covered in mud, grass and red flower petals.

"I look fine!"

"No, you don't," Helga said. She hoisted Vulgar up with one hand and marched in the direction of the duck pond in the back garden.

"But you will soon."

"You wouldn't!" Vulgar gulped.

SPLASH!

"Oh," he said, shivering in the cold water.

"You would."

81

CHAPTER SIX

GET THE PARTY STARTED

The Midsummer's Eve celebrations were in full swing when Vulgar arrived at the Great Hall. His skin had been scrubbed until it was bright pink, his hair had been brushed – even his clothes had been cleaned and dried. Helga had actually sat on them for a while to flatten out most of the creases.

Musicians were playing gentle melodies

on flutes and horns. The whole village
was gathered outside the Great Hall,
tucking into finger foods and filling up
jugs of mead from a big barrel. Vulgar
couldn't imagine any evil spirits being
scared away by mini reindeer sausages
and flute music.

He went in search of the bonfire. It took
him a while because he'd been expecting
to see a huge towering inferno spitting
clouds of black smoke into the sky.
Instead it was more like a small campfire.
Vulgar sighed. Only in Blubber could
they make something so brilliant into
something so boring.

Knut was the only person
standing by the fire. He looked
just as disappointed as Vulgar.

"What happened?"
Vulgar asked. "We
gathered loads of wood."

83

"The grown-ups said that this was big enough," Knut explained. "They said the bonfire isn't really the important bit anyway."

"It's the *most* important bit!" Vulgar said. "Grown-ups have no idea." He looked over at the buffet table, where the adults were chatting. They were gobbling whale-meat morsels and guzzling mead and not paying any attention to the bonfire. "We need to find more wood to build it up."

Knut glanced around the square. "Where from? It's too far to go back to the woods."

"There must be something we can burn," Vulgar said, scanning the party for something to use. "Hmm. The table's wooden... but they'd notice if we burned that." His eyes fell on a tall, thin log propped up against the side of a hut, a short distance away from the revellers. "There! That's perfect. Help me carry it."

The log was heavier than it looked. The villagers took no notice as the boys slowly dragged it over to the fire.

"Maybe we should ask permission first," Knut said nervously.

"Why? We're doing them a favour," Vulgar said. "This pathetic little campfire wouldn't even scare the tiniest pixie away." Hooking his arms underneath the log, he said, "Ready?" Knut nodded, his face red with the effort of holding his end up. "OK, one… two… three…"

They rolled the log into the flames and the fire

roared, forcing them to take a big jump backwards. The boys looked up at the blaze and grinned. "Now that's more like it," Vulgar said. "That won't just scare evil spirits out of Blubber, it'll scare them out of the whole country!"

A scream split the evening air around them. "My maypole! What have you done to my beautiful maypole?"

Vulgar recognised Freya's voice. "Uh-oh." He peered into the fire and noticed the strands of ribbon tied around the top of the burning log. "You know, I thought it looked a bit familiar," he muttered.

This wasn't good. Thinking fast, Vulgar ran and grabbed a big jug of mead and threw it towards the flames. In his panic, though, he missed and flung the jug's contents into Freya's face instead. The princess spluttered and gasped.

"Oops," Vulgar said, giggling

nervously. "Accident!"

Freya advanced menacingly, her blonde hair sticking to her wet face. Vulgar backed away through the crowd, trying to keep his distance. Freya was good at fighting. *Angry* Freya was unstoppable.

Vulgar backed up until he was trapped against the mead barrel. There were people on all sides. He had nowhere else to run!

With an angry cry, Freya shoved him backwards. He stumbled against the mead barrel. Boy and barrel both fell together. The mead *glugged* out over Vulgar, soaking him through for the second time that day.

Freya scowled down at him. "Oops," she growled. "Accident."

Now that they couldn't refill their jugs of mead, the grown-ups finally

noticed what was going on. And they didn't look happy. As Vulgar wrung out his tunic, the grown-ups ran, shouting, to the bonfire. Harald tipped his jug of mead on the flames. Helga fanned at the fire with her skirts. But the bonfire continued to blaze.

"Mind yer backs, you lot. Blubber fire department comin' through!" shouted Harrumf, hobbling past with a bucket of water. *SPLOSH!* The water sizzled on the flames, but still the inferno roared.

I'm soaking wet and I'll probably be grounded until I've grown a beard, thought Vulgar, *but at least I won't have to dance around the maypole.*

A hush fell over the crowd as they stood gazing at the leaping flames. Harrumf noisily cleared his throat. "It's time for the traditional maypole dance, only we ain't got a maypole no more on account of it bein' set on fire."

Freya burst into noisy sobs. Vulgar would have felt sorry for her if he hadn't felt so relieved.

King Olaf stepped up and elbowed Harrumf out of the way. "What the steward means to say is that… um… our Midsummer King and Queen will dance around the fire instead this year."

The crowd cheered. Vulgar suddenly perked up. Dancing around a bonfire was something a proper Viking would do!

"And we can all join in!"

The crowd cheered a second time, Vulgar hollering loudest of all. But as he started to jig with excitement, he felt a firm hand clamp down on his shoulder.

"Get out of those wet clothes or you'll catch your death of cold," Helga told him. Vulgar knew there was no use arguing with his mother – she could wrestle him out of his tunic with one hand tied behind her back. He wriggled out of his sodden clothes and heard someone giggle.

"I see Denmark, I see France, I see Vulgar's underpants," Freya sang as she adjusted her soggy flower crown.

Vulgar blushed as he stood there in his pants. Luckily the bonfire was still roaring, and the heat was keeping him toasty and warm.

The musicians struck up a new tune.

This one was faster and louder with a thudding drumbeat. The villagers began to dance around the fire. Tapping his toes to the rhythm, Vulgar saw his mum twirling around it, spinning his dad above her head. His dad *whummed* just like Vulgar's stick had done. King Olaf whirled around the bonfire merrily, his enormous belly bobbing up and down as he danced.

The music got faster still, and now even Harrumf couldn't resist the beat. The old man shuffled around the fire, beating his walking stick in time to the music.

"Join in, King Vulgar," Freya shouted as she skipped past. Vulgar hopped from foot to foot, then fell into step behind

Freya. Round and round they danced,
faster and faster, like Viking warriors
celebrating a victory. Vulgar whooped
wildly, good and loud to scare away those
pesky evil spirits.

All night long, the villagers cheered and
stomped and hollered and clapped. It was
the best Midsummer's Eve ever, and if the
elves and ogres and trolls had any sense,
Vulgar thought, they would stay far
away from the village of Blubber!